Praise for Storyshares

"One of the brightest innovators and game-changers in the education industry."
— Forbes

"Your success in applying research-validated practices to promote literacy serves as a valuable model for other organizations seeking to create evidence-based literacy programs." — Library of Congress

"We need powerful social and educational innovation, and Storyshares is breaking new ground. The organization addresses critical problems facing our students and teachers. I am excited about the strategies it brings to the collective work of making sure every student has an equal chance in life."
— Teach For America

"It's the perfect idea. There's really nothing like this. I mean, wow, this will be a wonderful experience for young people." — Andrea Davis Pinkney,
Executive Director, Scholastic

"Reading for meaning opens opportunities for a lifetime of learning. Providing emerging readers with engaging texts that are designed to offer both challenges and support for each individual will improve their lives for years to come. Storyshares is a wonderful start." — David Rose, Co-founder of CAST & UDL

What Would You Do?

Storyshares presents

Published by Storyshares, LLC

Storyshares
Storyshares, LLC
24 N. Bryn Mawr Avenue #340
Bryn Mawr, Pennsylvania 19010-3304
www.storyshares.org

Inspiring reading with a new kind of book.

Interest Level: Post-High School
Grade-Level Equivalent: 3.6

ISBN 9798885977241
Book design by Saskia Globig

What Would You Do?

a story about life and love

Stephen Leitschuh

Storyshares

contents

part one

What Would You Do to Be Less Selfish?

chapter one

Hi, my name is Craig and I'm a selfish loser.

It sounds like the opening line at a rehab meeting, doesn't it? But it's the cleaner version of what my ex-girlfriend Monica called me when she walked out.

"Craig, you are a pathetic, prideful, self-centered ass," were her exact words. The worst thing is that she was right.

"Please don't go. I can change," I said, begging her to stay. "Give me one more chance. If I screw up, I'll even help you pack."

"Craig, you really are clueless. Look around.

I already moved all my stuff out, if you haven't noticed. Besides, I'm sick and tired of hearing your sorry excuses. It's the same old crap you've been using since last year, six months ago, last month, and tonight.

"I just don't believe you anymore. It's always 'me, me, me.' Whatever happened to us? The only reason I'm even here right now is because I have enough class to break up in person instead of over text."

She stared at me. "Look at me, Craig. You just lost the best thing you will ever have."

Then she spun around and walked to the door.

I made one more final plea. "Monica, please. I promise I can change."

She never turned around as she stormed out the door.

chapter two

Did I like Monica? No, I loved her. I had been too stupid to admit it, even to myself, until now. Monica was right. She was the best thing that ever happened to me. She had a strange gift for helping me to be sensible and honest. I guess she grew tired of babysitting me.

Besides Monica being beautiful and having a great personality, each of my friends liked her. So, after she left, I did what every loser does. I got drunk—wildly drunk.

The next two weeks were a blur. Thank God my boss liked me, and I was good at my job. Otherwise, he would have fired me after the first week. He felt sorry for me, but like everyone else, he had his own problems to worry about.

Only one thing made me understand how bad losing Monica would be. It was the fact that all of my friends were her friends. They only put up with me for her sake. No one wanted to hang out with me or even stop for a drink after work anymore.

"I don't need them," I told myself.

I was at our usual bar alone for the countless night in a row. I was losing control over my life fast. If it wasn't for my one good friend, who was also my running partner, I would have had no one.

"Craig, get your sorry ass up!" Dan yelled. He pounded on my apartment door at six in the morning.

I flung open the door. "You want to get me kicked out of this place? I'm up already," I said, still wearing my boxers.

"Craig, you look like crap. Are you still drunk?" Dan asked. He pushed past me into the apartment. "Don't even think you're leaving me all alone again this morning. Get your ass dressed. You have five minutes."

chapter three

Dan and I took it pretty easy the first two miles. Then he picked up the pace.

"Are you trying to kill me? Have you no respect for how sick I am?" I yelled, struggling to keep up with him.

"Hey, man, I didn't pour those drinks down your throat last night. I was sober and in bed by ten with Diane." He smiled. "I'll take her over a six-pack of Corona any day of the week."

He laughed and picked up the pace again.

I stopped and puked. I half expected to see a kidney or lung lying on the ground. I wiped my face with my handkerchief before throwing it on the pile of slop on the ground.

I never caught up to Dan. He waited for me at my apartment, sipping on a bottle of water while I finished.

"Maybe tonight, you'll go a little easier on the sauce." He handed me what was left of his water. "I expect you to be up waiting for me tomorrow morning," he said, sliding into his car.

I dumped what little was left in the water bottle over my head and shook off the rest. I skipped breakfast. A cup of black coffee was all I had until I ate a bowl of mac and cheese at lunch. It was all I dared to eat, since throwing up at your desk was frowned upon.

Instead of stopping after work for a few beers, I quit drinking for a while. It was time to mature and act my age.

I must have been stronger than I thought. I went an entire month with nothing stronger than cream soda. Dan still kicked my butt on our morning runs, but at least I kept up with him now.

chapter four

"Hi, Mom, just checking in," I said. "Anything new?"

I already knew what was new. I always kept an upbeat tone in my voice when I called home each week.

"Hi, honey, not much is new here. Your father still threatens to move us all down to Florida with you. He says he's tired of the snow and cold weather up here," she laughed. "Since he doesn't golf or fish anymore, I keep telling him he would drive us nuts within a month."

"How's Gary doing?" I asked, already knowing the answer.

"He's better. He has his good days and bad days. You know how it is."

My younger brother Gary was sick again. He had been in and out of the hospital since he was a baby. He battled kidney disease for the first 18 years of his life and finally beat it. Now, he wasn't feeling good again.

I used to watch my mother lay out his pills every night. She carefully counted each one she took from one of the half dozen bottles. They kept him alive, but taking those high doses for so many years affected all of his joints. Doctors told Gary by the time he turned 30, he would probably need to have his knees and hips replaced if he wanted to keep walking.

To talk to him, you would never know he had ever been sick a day in his life. He exercised, played sports, and even went hunting and fishing. Hell, he did ten times more than me. Gary even found himself a girl and married her two years ago. Now, Brenda was pregnant with their first child. Unlike me, he had his life together.

"I'll call him this weekend and see how he and Brenda are doing. I might even sneak up to see you guys now that the snow is gone, if I can get away," I said.

I knew it probably wouldn't happen. At least it made my mom feel good that she might have the whole family together for a couple of days this summer.

"Mom, I have to go for now. I'll keep in touch. If anything comes up, let me know."

chapter five

Life went on. I slept, ate, worked, and got my butt kicked by Dan five days a week. I dated a few girls. Either we didn't click or they quickly tired of my attitude.

I saw Monica around and even talked to her once in a while, but I couldn't tell if she was dating. Without asking, I knew she would never date me ever again.

The week after the loneliest birthday I ever spent, my dad called me. "Craig, I have some bad news. Your brother has cancer. Lung cancer, to be exact."

"That's impossible! Gary never smoked a cigarette in his entire life."

"The doctors aren't sure how he got it. They just know it's a type you get from secondhand smoke. Maybe he got it from working at those sports bars when he was in college. The how really doesn't matter at this point.

"I also found out that when he switched jobs last year, because of his past kidney problems, he had to wait 12 months before getting his major medical coverage. Now he's screwed, and the insurance company won't stick up for him either."

"I thought he was on Brenda's insurance?" I asked.

"Because of his pre-existing condition, her insurance company wouldn't let her add him. They figured by the end of the year, he would be covered again."

"Are you saying he has no major medical insurance coverage?"

"Pretty much. They'll cover his prescriptions and general office visits, but nothing dealing with his cancer."

chapter six

My dad and I sat in a silence for a while. I tried to understand what this all meant for Gary.

"Dad... just how bad is it?"

"It's in the early stages. Thankfully, it's not a super aggressive type. They'll start radiation to see if they can shrink it. If not, they'll have to cut it out, and he'll have to go through chemo. The doctor says his chances are better than 75 percent because they caught it so early, but the costs will be expensive."

"I don't have a lot saved up, but Gary's more than welcome to it."

"It's going to take a lot more than you, me, Gary,

and Brenda can ever come up with. The 48 radiation sessions alone are over $30,000.

"Gary and Brenda are still fighting with the insurance company and looking for a hospital that will work with them. But Gary doesn't have a lot of time. He needs to start treatment in no more than two months.

"Look, we haven't told your mom yet because she will do nothing but worry. Gary didn't even want me to call you. If you talk to him, don't mention it unless he tells you himself. I'm sorry it couldn't be better news, but I thought you should know. I'll e-mail you updates when I hear more. If you get the chance, call him this weekend. He and Brenda are feeling a little low right now."

We said goodbye and hung up. *Feeling a little low?* I thought. *Damn, I'd be going crazy right about now.*

I pulled up my bank account online. I figured I had about $5,000 extra and could send Gary maybe an extra couple hundred every month, but Dad was right. It was far off from $30,000.

I called my brother on Sunday. Neither he nor Brenda said anything about his condition. They told me they were looking forward to the baby, summer vacation, and finishing the renovations on their house. I almost said something, but respected my dad's wishes.

chapter seven

I spent the next week on the computer researching all there was to know about lung cancer. I looked up costs and if anyone was doing any cutting-edge research who Gary could connect with. There was one place in Chicago. The only catch was Gary and Brenda would have to move there to qualify.

The Mayo Clinic in Rochester, Minnesota, had nothing. Most of the small hospitals' budgets were too tight to do much for him. I couldn't believe with all the money the insurance companies made that they couldn't help him.

My first ray of hope came from the American Cancer Society. I had raised money for them over the years, especially when a close friend of mine died of ovarian cancer. After beating breast cancer, she was diagnosed with stage four ovarian cancer. She died in less than a month. I think she lost hope.

I would not let that to happen to my brother.

I spoke to a kind lady named Fran from the Cancer Society's local office. Their current funds were already claimed. However, Fran said I could still raise money for my brother under the ACS label. She gave me written permission and wished me the best of luck.

"If there is anything we can do, let us know. The more it's out there in the news, the more donations we receive," Fran said.

Thursday morning, Dan came up with the idea of a cancer run fundraiser. "Hell, we'll get people to donate so much a mile like they do for the Relay For Life fundraisers. Then, all you have to do is run or walk and collect the money—easy."

However, when I asked for donations, I saw just how difficult it would be. A dollar a mile was the best I could get from anyone. I had 20 sponsors and figured at this rate, it would take 5,000 to get the money Gary needed. Worst of all, I was running out of time.

That's when I turned off the common sense button in my brain.

chapter eight

It took me another week to make my initial plans.
I came up with a crazily absurd plan to walk from
my apartment in Orlando, Florida, to the Mayo Clinic in Rochester, Minnesota. Then I'd give them a
check for my brother's treatment.

When I talked to new sponsors, they just rolled
their eyes. They said if I was going to attempt it,
they would support me. Things were looking up.

"Are you drunk or crazy?" Dan demanded. We
walked back to my apartment after our morning run.
"There is no way you can do it. Physically, it's just
impossible. Have you even talked to your job about

it? Do you have any idea how long that's going to take you?"

He kept yelling while he peppered me with questions on why it couldn't be done. He was probably right, but I didn't have another plan and I was running out of time.

"Dan, look at it this way. I'm in great shape. If nothing else, I can run, walk, and even crawl my way there. Two years ago, I ran 61 miles in a day and didn't even get a blister on my feet. I know it's a long way, but it's for my only brother. What choice do I have?"

"All right, I'll help you set it up," Dan said. He tried to stare me down. "I just want you to know up front, you will never make it."

Never tell me I can't do something. It's like waving a red flag in front of a bull.

chapter nine

Dan and I spent the next two weeks planning out my insane idea.

My boss understood my problem and talked to corporate for me. I could take the three weeks of vacation days I had saved up. The company let me add in the ten paid holidays. They told me we would work out the details later.

They also pledged a dollar a mile. That gave me 31 total days, 25 of which were paid. My company also gave me the option of another ten extra days of unpaid leave. That gave me 41 days. Hell, no way it would take me that long.

Saturday, I stopped at our local running store. Like everyone else, they rolled their eyes. Still, they agreed to give me five pairs of running shoes, as long as they could put their name on the shoes. They even let me hang a poster for pledges on their activity board.

"If you make it, I want a pair of your shoes to put on display," the owner said. "It'll inspire new runners for what's possible."

Next, I had to find a large hotel chain. Then, no matter which town I ended up in, I would have a place to stay. The Holiday Inns gave me a 50 percent discount on their cheapest room rate, which would not be more than $25 a night. They sent Dan a list of locations. We began to plan out my route.

Since I was our company's purchasing manager, they let me ask our vendors for donations. Of the 83 vendors, 27 said they would donate. One vendor told me I was a decimal place off in the distance I gave him. When I told them 1,100 miles was correct, they asked where they could send flowers and condolence cards.

They laughed. I didn't.

chapter ten

Being a Harley rider, I visited the dealership where I had purchased my last two bikes. They asked if I had taken a recent fall. They figured I'd hit my head when I told them my plan.

"Look, all I'm asking is for a pledge of anything you can give me per mile and ten t-shirts. I will put them in each of the ten dealerships in the Tri-county area. People can donate and write on the shirt the name of someone they know that has or had cancer. I know the shirts sponsor rides and fundraisers, but this way they would also get a little advertisement, since I will wear them every day."

They thought I was crazy but gave me the shirts and contacted the other dealerships, who also pledged.

It was all coming together.

I spent a week laying out clothes and medical supplies. I would need a minimum number of calories per day to keep up my strength. I would also need to stop for lunch every day. I didn't want to carry a lot of money with me, so I planned to rely on my credit and debit cards to pay for everything.

"Craig, you will never be able to carry all this stuff," Dan said, looking at my pile. "Maybe, just maybe, I have a solution."

The next day he came back with a tiny two-wheel plastic cart. "You can put everything into dry bags and pull it behind you." He showed me the harness he made for me to pull it. "It's going to slow you down a bit, but at least you will have everything with you in case you run into a problem."

We tried it the next day on our morning run. I didn't like it, but I had little choice.

chapter eleven

From start to finish, it took me three-and-a-half
weeks to plan my quest. I had my iPhone with a
GPS app and a roaming Internet connection to
keep me on track. It would also tell me how far
I had run each day. From my iTunes library, I load-
ed up my old iPod with every song I could imagine.
Finally, I put my map route into both my phone and
daily planner. I chose May 1st as my starting date.

To the various hotels I would stay at, I mailed
t-shirts, four pairs of socks, and two pairs of running shorts. I sent my extra running shoes to a few

places along the way so I would have a fresh pair every week. I figured my feet would be my main concern if I ever expected to finish.

"Craig, I thought you gave up the booze!" my dad said the day before I left.

"I did, but kind of wish I hadn't right about now. I have at least 55 sponsors. If everything goes as planned, I should raise a little over $40,000."

"What's your best estimate on the number of miles to the Mayo Clinic?"

"It's not a straight route from Orlando to Rochester. So my best guess is just over 1,100 miles, give or take."

My dad whistled. "That's a long way by car, much less walking."

"I'm hoping to average 35 to 40 miles a day. Easy," I told him.

"I just hope you know what you're doing."

"Dad, I'm not even sure about it myself. I have only one brother and no other way to raise money as fast as he needs it. Just don't tell Gary or Mom. She'll worry, and Gary will try to talk me out of it like everyone else. I should see you in about 40 days. I'll have my phone with me, so call if you need me."

"I love you, son," was the last thing he said before he hung up.

Dan showed up the next morning just before I took off.

"Maybe this will help." He taped a little sign on the back of my cart: *Florida to Minnesota Cancer Run. Donations welcome.* "It might help. It sure as hell can't hurt. I'm also going to call all your friends to see if they will pledge anything," he said.

"Friends? Hell, that should get me all of a dollar fifty," I said with a laugh.

So, on a beautiful, warm May morning, I took off on a quest to help my brother. I didn't have a clue what I was in for, but I sure as hell couldn't back out now.

part two

What Would You Do to Save a Life?

chapter one

I blew past my first night motel stop, making almost 58 miles on the first day. Thankfully, I hadn't sent any spare clothing to that motel. If I didn't have to pull that damn cart, I probably could have done five to seven more miles.

I felt pretty cocky when I checked into the next motel on the list a day early. I removed my soaked Harley t-shirt. I washed it in the bathroom sink, along with my socks and shorts. The hot shower felt heavenly.

I threw my wet clothes over the shower rod to dry. I looked at the 38 names of people who had cancer written on the shirt. I would switch to a fresh shirt each day and rotate my shoes. My main goal was to keep my feet clean and dry.

I grabbed a quick dinner at a Denny's. After watching a little television, I went to bed. I didn't set an alarm. I figured I would let my body choose my pace. After a breakfast of scrambled eggs and sausage links, I was off again. I called Fran and told her I had started my quest and would check in with her twice a week.

I felt a little sore, but after popping two ibuprofen, it got a little better. People honked. A few threw me dollar bills as I ran. Every town I stopped in, I checked for a Harley dealership. Most pledged something or gave me an extra shirt to wear.

I heard that all the local dealerships back home had hung large maps and plotted my daily progress on them. I also heard there was a bet going on about how long I would last. The big money was on 22 days.

chapter two

I had to stop walking on day six after only 21 miles. My feet were burning with pain. I emptied two bags of ice into the bathtub, took a deep breath, and shoved in both feet. The pain was instant. I thought ice was supposed to make them feel better.

I did my best not to cry and decided that I was pushing myself a little too hard. I would have to back off a little before I ran out of energy and quit.

I picked up some diaper rash ointment and a box of round band aids for my nipples. They were already rubbed raw and bleeding. I had averaged 45 miles a day and needed to rest for a day or two before pushing it again.

I had been using the two-ten strategy. I jogged for two minutes and walked for ten. When I found that walking hurt my feet more than jogging, I revised it to jog for ten minutes and walk for three. It wasn't perfect but worked for the next few days.

Dan was right. I wasn't in as good shape as I thought. Running five to seven miles for five days a week was one thing. Even running a marathon was impressive. This went way beyond that. At day ten, my legs felt like lead. Worst of all, my iPod got wet and stopped working.

The next day, I doubled up on my socks when I saw the start of a nasty blister on the heel of my left foot. My body had started to fall apart.

The worst part was the loneliness of being out there by myself. I had a lot of time to think and reflect on my life. After thinking about the last two years, I realized Monica was right. I truly was a self-centered ass.

I only helped others when I absolutely had to, but expected everyone to drop what they were doing to help me.

I made a mental note to call Monica when I got back. Maybe I could get her to at least talk to me.

chapter three

Two and a half weeks in, Fran told me she had col-
lected $2,000 for my brother.

"I don't understand. I thought all your funds
were claimed," I said.

"I let the local news know what you're doing.
Now, they're giving updates on where you are and
how you're doing. . . Craig, how are you doing?"

"In two words, sore and tired. But it looks like
I can't quit now even if I wanted to," I said with a
forced laugh. "I'm pushing for June 12th. I only
hope my feet and legs last that long."

"Well, keep up the good work. Remember, it's

for your brother."

She didn't have to say that. I already knew it. I just hoped I could make it without dying in the process.

Why didn't I just say 250 or 500 miles? That would have made a lot more sense.

I kept walking.

I wrote in my journal every day. I wrote about how I was doing, feeling, and if anything exciting happened.

On day 20, a car stopped next to me and a man handed me a one-hundred-dollar bill.

On day 23, a little old lady waited for me along the road. She gave me a bag of cookies and a ten-dollar bill. "God bless," was all she said.

On day 29, it rained all day. I was soaked from eight in the morning until six at night. I was freezing cold and thought I would lose it before I made it to the hotel for a hot shower.

Like most nights, I iced my feet on and off for the better part of an hour. Then I put on lotion and baby powder. I logged my miles and, for the first time since I began, I had doubts.

chapter four

I slept with my feet propped up on two pillows to reduce the swelling. In the mornings now, I took a hot bath to get the blood flowing in my legs.

The ultra-marathoner Dan Jansen had run 30 marathons in 30 days the previous year. I read his articles on what he ate and everything else he did to prepare for those runs. I soon realized I was no Dan Jansen.

By the way my shorts now fit, I could tell I had lost weight. I hadn't counted on burning as many calories as I was. Even though I was exhausted by the end of the day, I had to force myself to eat.

I was sick of eggs for breakfast, but they were easy, fast, and stayed down. My lunch usually included Gatorade, granola bars, and fruit. I tried to eat a bowl of pasta and a big hunk of meat every night. I needed the carbs and protein to keep my energy levels up.

Jackie, my second-in-command at work, updated me on what was happening. Over the phone, we solved the day-to-day problems. She became my first call of the day. I think Jackie did it to take my mind off of the pain. I felt it every morning the instant my feet hit the floor.

Days 31 through 35 were awful. I slowed down. My feet hurt all the time. The muscles in both calves always knotted up. My quads burned with each step.

The blister on my left heel was the size of a silver dollar, and I had small ones on the balls of each foot. Both of my big toenails were now black, and all my toes looked like little red sausages.

Every night, after I iced my feet, I drained the blisters, smeared on a glob of Neosporin, and covered them with large bandages. I started limping to take the weight off of my sore left foot and even tried to jog on the balls of my feet whenever I felt brave enough.

chapter five

Day 37 was cold, with a constant misty rain. I started off with a raincoat and hat. Then I added rain-
proof bottoms when I got cold. At about six o'clock,
I came up on two guys with a microphone and
camera.

"Craig, can I talk to you for a couple of minutes?" the guy with the microphone asked. He
shoved it in my face.

I was thankful for the break. I told him why I was
on my quest and how disgusted I was with the insurance companies, hospitals, and even the politi-

cians.

"I would love to have a couple of executives in their corporate ivory towers get really sick and have the insurance companies tell them they aren't covered. I think you would see changes overnight instead of having to wait for years. Meanwhile, the little people get screwed over.

"If insurance companies just stopped arguing with each other and thought about the average person who pays taxes and can't afford to get sick, maybe they would do something. But it all comes down to money: those who have it and those who need it. It makes me sick. So I walk to give my brother what he can't get on his own. It just isn't fair."

"Craig, do you think you will finish?"

"I don't have a choice. I'm not a doctor who can treat him. I don't own a hospital. I sure as hell don't run an insurance company. If I did, I wouldn't have to do what I'm doing right now.

"My brother needs treatment. I will do whatever is necessary to see that he gets it. Thank you for listening. If you will excuse me, I need to keep moving before my legs tighten up, or I will never finish."

The cameraman panned out to catch me limping away. That was how they ended the piece.

chapter six

On day 40, my dad called to tell me Mom and Gary found out about my plan.

"They're angry that no one told them what you were up to. Someone saw the news clip and called Gary, who called your Mom. She's angry I kept it from her. Gary wants to know where the hell you are now."

"Tell them I will see them in a couple of days," I said, and forced myself to keep moving.

I just wanted this nightmare to end. At this point, it hurt to even breathe. Forget jogging. I struggled to walk.

I remember someone telling me that when all else fails, just put one foot in front of the other and keep moving. That's exactly what I did. Now, at night, after icing my feet, I called and had my dinner delivered. I didn't want to do anything but stay off my feet.

I was slowing down to a crawl. I couldn't do anything besides put in longer hours, which meant the pain lasted longer and longer every day. I was popping about five to seven ibuprofen a day, and my stomach felt the effects.

At day 47, I almost lost it. I was just a little over a mile from the motel. When I sat down to tie my shoe, my muscles tightened up, and I couldn't get back up. I had the hotel send an Uber to get me.

I cried for the first time that night. Not for me, but for my brother. I was so close. I had to finish.

I now wrapped my feet in elastic bandages to keep the swelling down. When I stopped for lunch, I bought a bag of ice and laid it on top of the bandages. My toes had started bleeding and, for the past three days, I had put gauze between my toes so they wouldn't rub together.

My feet were one big blister, but I was finally in Minnesota. I could see the finish.

chapter seven

I woke up on day 49 to three local news reporters outside my door. They gave me coffee and donuts and spent 20 minutes talking through it all again. Most of the fight was out of me by now.

Fran had sent a check for $9,000 dollars to the Mayo Clinic. When one reporter asked if I had raised enough money, I told them I wasn't sure.

"I did my best. That's all I can do. Over the last several months, I learned a lot about the health care system and how it should be changed. It all comes down to helping people."

I looked the reporter straight in the eyes and asked him, "What would you do to save a life? Your sister, wife, mother, brother, daughter? How far would you go?

"Then ask the insurance company that same question. Make them give you an answer in dollars and cents because that's what it's all about. They are not gods, yet they still hold your life in their hands. I ask you, what does that say about our health care system?"

"Craig, have you always been a fighter for the rights of the underdogs?" another reporter asked me.

"A girl who I foolishly let get away told me I was a self-centered ass who would never change. I thought she was right for a long time. Eventually, I realized people can change if they really want to. So, if I can change from a selfish idiot into a person on a mission, can you imagine what a big insurance company can do?"

I grabbed one more cup of coffee and thanked them for their time. I told them I had two more days left and would answer all questions after that.

chapter eight

The next morning started the longest two days of my life.

My dad said everyone would meet me at the Mayo Clinic. He wanted me to let him know when I was close. Then he would tell everyone. At one time, I thought I would jog the last day and show everyone just how tough I was, but the pain was way too severe for such foolishness.

It felt like needles were sticking me with every step and every muscle was paying me back for pushing them beyond their limit. My feet were a bloody mess. My legs weren't much better. But I was close. That was the only thing that kept me putting one foot in front of the other.

I had gotten little sleep the last couple of nights because my legs ached all the time. When I finished at night, I would lie in a hot bath until the water got cold. Then I drained it and started all over again.

Being on my feet for 14 to 16 hours a day meant there weren't enough hours left for a full night's sleep.

15 miles were all I had left on the last day. I started at eight in the morning, figuring it would probably take me at least ten to twelve hours. I called Fran to say it was almost over, and I appreciated all her support.

Jackie and I talked for the last time. I told her I would see her on Monday morning. "I might be in a wheelchair, but I will be there."

She laughed and told me to just shut up and finish because she was tired of carrying my ass at work. I would have laughed too, except I was just too tired.

My body was exhausted. I was ready to crash at any moment.

chapter nine

I called my dad to give him an idea of where I was and how long I thought I would be. At five miles to go, I saw my brother leaning against a telephone pole waiting for me.

"You look like crap. Couldn't you at least have shaved this morning and put on clean clothes?" he asked, with a forced smile.

"Been a little busy, if you haven't noticed," I said.

"Yeah, yeah, you always were a whiner. Come on. Pick up your damn feet and let's get moving. Mom said not to be late. We're having dinner at her house tonight."

I was too tired even to smile.

At three miles left, I started to tear up. I stumbled on a curb because I couldn't raise my foot high enough and almost fell. I just wanted the pain to go away.

Gary begged me to stop or at least let him help me, but I told him I had come this far and I was going to finish.

"For once in my life, I will finish what I started," I told him. But mostly I told myself.

At one mile left, I was shuffling. My body knew I was almost there and slowed down. If Gary hadn't been by my side, I don't think I would have made it. I shuffled like a 90-year-old man and had tears in my eyes from the pain.

chapter ten

When I saw the hospital, I lost it. Tears ran down my cheeks. My legs began shaking. *Walk, damn it!* my brain said as I pushed my legs beyond their limit once more.

The sidewalk up to the front entrance inclined at what must have been 30 degrees.

Who in the hell would put a hospital on a damn hill?

Then I heard it.

It wasn't loud at first, but grew louder as I came closer. With my head down, fighting for every step, I looked up. About 50 people were cheering at the entrance. I stopped, took a deep breath, straightened, and walked the last hundred feet with my head held high, right into my dad's arms.

They had a gurney waiting and eased me onto it while everyone cheered and congratulated me. They whisked me into the emergency room where two doctors waited.

They cut off my shoes and the elastic bandages and surveyed the damage. I was right. My feet were a mess. The doctors cleaned and bandaged my feet. They said I had to stay off of them for at least two to three weeks, so I guess I was right about the wheelchair. With an IV needle in my arm and my family around my bedside, it was finally over.

part three

What Would You Do to Prove Your Love?

chapter one

I received a free ambulance ride to my parents'
house and a wheelchair to use for a couple of days.

I asked that they not make a fuss, but it seemed
like no one listened to me anymore. All my old
friends and family were there. Everyone told me
how proud they were. I thanked them, but I was
glad when they left. Mom told them she would keep
them updated.

I ate more for dinner than I had in weeks. By
seven o'clock, I struggled to stay awake.

A bath—no way could I stand in the shower—and
a shave sitting in the tub brought me a little relief.

But I needed sleep, and lots of it. Two pain pills and I was out like a light, sleeping in my old bedroom.

Even though the room was dark, I knew it had to be at least midday when I opened my eyes. My body had been waking me up naturally at five for too long. This morning, I knew something was different. I felt numb and a little fuzzy in the head as I tried to sit up and get out of bed.

This will not be fun, I thought.

I looked at my two wrapped-up stumps. I howled when I tried to put my weight down on one foot before climbing back onto the bed. The pain was back with a vengeance.

Using a crutch, I slid my wheelchair over to the side of the bed and hopped in. Going to the bathroom was not easy. I moved myself onto the toilet, back into the wheelchair, and brushed my teeth without soaking myself or the entire floor.

I threw on an old sweatshirt and wheeled myself out of the bedroom and into the kitchen. Everyone sat around the kitchen table, quietly drinking coffee. They had been waiting for me to wake up.

chapter two

When I asked if there was any coffee left, the kitchen sprang to life.

"Before you ask, yes, I slept well," I said. "I am still lightheaded. And no, I can't walk. Besides that, I'm doing pretty well."

"Well, I'm glad you're up. Your cell phone has been ringing nonstop. Finally, I had to turn it off. I was afraid it would wake you," my dad told me. He slipped a cup of coffee under my nose.

"Nothing could have woken me last night after two of those pills. The only reason I'm up now is that my bladder decided I had slept enough."

"So, Craig, tell me. What are your plans for today?" my brother asked. "I thought we might go out and jog a few laps around the football field just to stay active. I wouldn't want you to get lazy on me."

I smirked at him. "Besides buying plane tickets for tomorrow, I want to do nothing today. My only problem will be moving around for a couple of weeks. There is no way I can walk, and I still have to work for a living. I guess I'll figure out something."

"It seems you don't have to worry about that, at least for now. Someone volunteered to be your wet nurse," Gary said. "Mom wanted to come down and do it, but we felt that her dragging your ass on and off the toilet and into the bath might be a little embarrassing for her," my brother said, trying not to laugh.

"For her? How about for me?"

"You haven't got anything she hasn't seen before," he replied. "But Mom was overruled."

That statement surprised even me. "Who the hell could overrule Mom? Dad hasn't even said crap to her in the last ten years."

Out of the corner of my eye, I saw my dad give me that look that said I needed to be careful.

chapter three

A voice from behind Brenda spoke up, "I did."

Monica stepped forward. "They figured since I've seen it all before and already live in Florida, I was the logical choice."

"This little one showed up on our doorstep two days ago and has been waiting for your sorry ass," Brenda told me. "I told her you weren't worth her time. Although she agreed with me, she talked us into letting her stay."

My eyes lit up, and my heart started pumping again when Monica walked up and gave me a soft kiss.

"I told you guys this would be just what he needed," a smiling Brenda told my parents. "Maybe we should let them catch up. Craig's probably still tired anyway."

She pushed everyone out of the kitchen, leaving Monica and I alone.

"I don't understand," I said.

"Me either. Dan was the one who told us about your little plan when he went asking for donations. We all thought it was one of your stupid pranks. But when we checked it out, we realized you were really trying to do this."

"Did do it," I corrected her.

"All right, did it. When you gave that first and then the second interview, we all felt terrible for what we said and put you through, even though you deserved it. Craig, no one, and I mean no one, thought you would make it besides Fran and Jackie. Everyone at the Harley dealership lost and donated their bets to you.

"I flew out here after your last interview. I tracked down your parents and met your brother and sister-in-law. Gary's really proud of what you did for him. He wanted to meet you at the Minnesota border, along with everyone else, but your dad told everyone to back off and let you do this on your own. I was wrong. It seems even you can grow up if you put your mind to it."

I didn't hear everything she said. I was too busy staring at her. She was really here. I wasn't dreaming it.

chapter four

"Earth to Craig, have you heard one word I just said?" Monica asked.

"We can talk later," I said, trying to stand up and grab her before I realized what the hell I was doing.

"This is going to be a lot harder than I thought," she said, pushing me back into my wheelchair. "In order for this to work, you will have to do everything I say. Understood?"

She crossed her arms over her chest. She wasn't kidding. She meant business.

"Understood. You are the boss."

"Okay. Now, you still need some rest."

She wheeled me back down the hall toward my old bedroom. Once inside, she locked the door and pushed the wheelchair next to the bed. I used my arms to lift myself up and slide onto the bed. She pulled the wheelchair away.

"I want you to get some sleep. Your face still looks a little green, and we fly home tomorrow afternoon. So lie down."

I did as ordered. "I need a kiss goodnight. I can't sleep without a kiss goodnight," I said, smiling at her.

"Okay, but only one. You need to build your strength back up. The doctor ordered sleep."

I waited until Monica leaned in close enough and then pulled her onto the bed next to me. "I know what the doctor ordered, and it wasn't sleep," I told her.

"Craig, not yet. We're going to take this slow because I don't want to be hurt again. I can't do that to myself."

"Monica, I will never do that again. I promise you. All I ask is for you to trust me enough to give me another chance. I'm not saying I'm perfect, but with you here to kick my butt when I mess up, I think we can make it."

She got her way. I went back to sleep, but not alone. We didn't do anything in my mom's house. We waited until Monday night when we got back to my apartment. I never realized how much you use feet in making love.

chapter five

If seeing Monica hadn't felt real before, it did on Sunday night. I overheard her on her cell phone when I was supposed to be asleep.

"No, I can't see you anymore. I'm back with my old boyfriend. . . . No, it wasn't anything you did. It's just that I want to give it another shot. That's all."

The last thing I heard was, "If it doesn't work out, I'll call you."

Do I dare bring it up to Monica? No. There was no way on this earth I would screw up our relationship this time. Maybe later I might ask her if she dated anyone after we broke up, and if so, how serious it was, but not now. Everything was still too new. We were happy, and I wanted to keep it that way.

Monday morning, Monica dropped me and my wheelchair off at work. Jackie met me at the door and wheeled me inside. A banner hung across my door that read "Welcome Back." The company and employees presented me with a check for $3,900 and even had a cake for me at lunch that said Florida to Minnesota or Bust.

I spent the better half of two weeks gathering donations. A few other vendors who saw the news clips also donated. Each of the Harley dealerships gave $1,000. Their corporate office in Milwaukee donated $3,000 on their own. Fran said my publicity had generated a lot of donations. If I was available, the regional manager wanted to meet me. Things were looking up.

Between Fran and I, we raised $62,000. But after my rants on the news, the Mayo Clinic paid the entire bill for Gary's treatment.

The best news came three months later. His radiation treatment shrank the tumor. He just needed a minor surgery to remove what was left. Gary had a couple of chemo sessions just to be safe.

After six months, he received a clean bill of health. Monica and I flew up two months after Brenda had her baby for our second homecoming in nine months.

Brenda and Gary wanted to name their baby after me, but I talked them out of it. "I'm no role model, not yet anyway. It would put too much pressure on me. Besides, what girl wants to be called Craig?"

chapter six

When we came back from Minnesota, Monica moved in only to help me. She slept on the couch bed for the next three weeks. When I could finally walk again, she stayed, but we were not an actual couple yet. She still wasn't ready to commit to me. Finally, just before Christmas, we officially became a couple.

On Christmas Eve, Monica gave me a new iPod Touch to replace the one I destroyed on my trip. I gave her an engagement ring. I think my present was better.

The ring surprised her. She thought we were still in the talking stage. I bought a gaudy ring with a huge plastic stone and put it in a box. I wrapped it and put a big bow on it.

She opened the box and gave me the look. It wasn't a happy one.

"What the hell is this?" she asked.

"It's a ring. Don't you like it? It may be a little big, so we'll probably need to get it sized," I said. I took it from her and squeezed the band to make it smaller so I could put it on her right hand. "Perfect," I said, holding her hand out.

I think she was about to say something ugly when I pulled the real ring out of my top shirt pocket and slipped it on her left hand.

"I guess if you don't like that one, maybe you'll like this one better."

I watched her eyes, hoping this time to get a different look.

Thankfully, her eyes lit up, and she gave me the hug and kiss I hoped for.

After looking at the ring, she turned to face me. "Asshole."

"You know, that's the same thing you said to me last time," I told her.

"Yeah, I know. This time, I mean it in a good way."

I pulled her over to me and said in a very serious voice, "Monica, will you give me the best Christmas present ever and become my wife?"

We were married four months later.

chapter seven

On our first anniversary, I asked the question I had wanted to ask Monica for well over a year and a half. "Monica, when we broke up, did you find or date someone else to replace me?"

She looked at me, smiled, and gave me a full mouth kiss.

"Are you talking about that phone call I made the Sunday night we first got back from Minnesota? The one where you pretended to be asleep? The one where I talked just loud enough to make sure you overheard every word I said? The call that took you all this time to ask about? What do you think?" she asked.

I stood there with a shocked look on my face.

"I dated a few guys, but found no one to replace you. But I couldn't let you know that. I figured that if you thought I had someone in the wings, you might try a little harder this time. It worked, didn't it?"

"That was evil," I replied.

"I'll show you just how evil I can be," she said, kissing me, and then ran towards the bedroom.

I walked toward our room. It had taken me almost 1,100 miles to prove to the woman I loved that I was worth a second chance. I would need all the strength I could muster to prove to her she had definitely made the right choice.

About the Author

Stephen Leitschuh is retired and living with his wife, Ilene, in sunny Florida. He began writing short stories when as a Marine, he was serving in Viet Nam. Being the third oldest of ten children, he had a lot of experiences to draw from. He has written everything from short stories to novels and received awards for his work from the Florida Writer's Association. "Writing is a way to live the life you dream of!"

About the Publisher

Storyshares is a publisher focused on supporting the millions of teens and adults who struggle with reading by creating a new shelf in the library specifically for them. The ever-growing collection features content that is compelling and culturally relevant for teens and adults, yet still readable at a range of lower reading levels.

Storyshares generates content by engaging deeply with writers, bringing together a community to create this new kind of book. With more intriguing and approachable stories to choose from, the teens and adults who have fallen behind are improving their skills and beginning to discover the joy of reading.

For more information, visit storyshares.org.

Easy to Read. Hard to Put Down.

www.ingramcontent.com/pod-product-compliance
Lightning Source LLC
Chambersburg PA
CBHW051312170626
46809CB00004B/1867